The Best Club

by Fran Manushkin

illustrated by Tammie Lyon

PICTURE WINDOW BOOKS
a capstone imprint

Katie Woo is published by Picture Window Books,
A Capstone Imprint
1710 Roe Crest Drive
North Mankato, Minnesota 56003
www.mycapstone.com

Text © 2017 Fran Manushkin
Illustrations © 2017 Picture Window Books

Library of Congress Cataloging-in-Publication Data
Names: Manushkin, Fran, author. | Lyon, Tammie, illustrator. |
   Manushkin, Fran. Katie Woo.
Title: The best club / by Fran Manushkin ; [illustrator, Tammie Lyon].
Description: North Mankato, Minnesota : Picture Window Books, an
   imprint of Capstone Press, 2016. | ©2017 | Series: Katie Woo | Summary:
   Katie Woo and her friends would love to be part of Sophie's new club, but
   Sophie does not think they, or anyone, is good enough, so they form their
   own club.
Identifiers: LCCN 2015046877| ISBN 9781479596393 (library binding) |
   ISBN 9781479596416 (pbk.) | ISBN 9781479596430 (ebook pdf)
Subjects: LCSH: Woo, Katie (Fictitious character)—Juvenile fiction. |
   Chinese Americans—Juvenile fiction. | Clubs—Juvenile fiction. |
   Friendship—Juvenile fiction. | CYAC: Chinese Americans—Fiction. |
   Clubs—Fiction. | Friendship—Fiction.
Classification: LCC PZ7.M3195 Bei 2016 | DDC 813.54—dc23
LC record available at http://lccn.loc.gov/2015046877

Graphic Designer: Heidi Thompson
Photo Credits:
Greg Holch, pg. 26
Tammie Lyon, pg. 26
Vector images, Shutterstock ©

Printed in the United States of America in North Mankato, Minnesota.
009665F16

Table of Contents

Chapter 1
Sophie's Club

Katie was talking to JoJo.

She said, "Wouldn't it be fun

to be in a club?"

"For sure!" said JoJo. "It

would be the best!"

Sophie Silver heard Katie
and JoJo.

"Guess what?" she said.
"I'm starting a club. It will
be the best."

"Wow!" said Katie. "Can I be in your club?"

"I will think about it," said Sophie. "You have to be the best."

"Oh," said Katie.

She began to worry.

Yoko Moto asked Sophie,

"Can I be in your club? I'm a

terrific artist."

"My paintings are better,"
said Sophie. "I don't think
you can be in my club."

At recess, Fatima Ford said,
"I can do three cartwheels. I
am the best!"

"No way," said Sophie. "I
can do four."

Fatima walked away,
looking sad.

Chapter 2

Best at Everything

Katie told JoJo, "It's hard to be in Sophie's club. But I know what to do. Sophie loves pretty clothes. I will wear mine tomorrow."

The next day, Katie ran

over to Sophie, saying, "Don't

I look great? Now can I be in

your club?"

"Sorry," said Sophie. "My

dresses are better."

Katie was sad all morning.

She kept looking at Sophie

and thinking.

Katie thought very hard.

At recess, JoJo told Sophie,

"I don't think anyone can be

the best at everything."

"Well, I am!" shouted

Sophie. "And you're not."

JoJo couldn't help it. She

began to cry.

Katie looked at Sophie
and said, "Sophie, you are
right. You are the best."

Sophie smiled.

Katie added, "You are the best at being mean! That's what you are!"

Sophie stopped smiling.

"Katie is right," said Yoko Moto. "Who would want to be in your club?"

"Nobody!" said JoJo. "Let's start our own club."

"That's the best idea," agreed Katie. "We will begin with a party! All the members can come."

"Yay!" yelled Fatima Ford and Yoko Moto.

They were so happy, they did four cartwheels.

Chapter 3
Katie's Secret

Sophie walked away. She looked sad. She looked sad all day.

After school, she got on the bus looking sad.

Katie sat down next to
Sophie. She told her, "I know
a secret."

Sophie looked at her.
"What secret?"

Katie whispered, "It's okay
if you are not the best."

"It is?" Sophie looked surprised.

"Yes." Katie smiled. "You just need to be yourself."

Sophie smiled back. "I can try that."

"It's easy," said JoJo. "I do it every day."

A few days later, Katie's club had their party.

They sang. They danced. They hugged. It was the best party ever!

About the Author

Fran Manushkin is the author of many popular picture books, including *Happy in Our Skin*; *Baby, Come Out!*; *Latkes and Applesauce: A Hanukkah Story*; *The Tushy Book*; *The Belly Book*; and *Big Girl Panties*. There is a real Katie Woo — she's Fran's great-niece — but she never gets in half the trouble of the Katie Woo in the books. Fran writes on her beloved Mac computer in New York City, without the help of her two naughty cats, Chaim and Goldy.

About the Illustrator

Tammie Lyon began her love for drawing at a young age while sitting at the kitchen table with her dad. She continued her love of art and eventually attended the Columbus College of Art and Design, where she earned a bachelor's degree in fine art. After a brief career as a professional ballet dancer, she decided to devote herself full time to illustration. Today she lives with her husband, Lee, in Cincinnati, Ohio. Her dogs, Gus and Dudley, keep her company as she works in her studio.

Glossary

artist (AR-tist)—someone very skilled at painting, making things, or performing in the arts

cartwheels (KART-wheelz)—circular, sideways handstands

recess (REE-sess)—a break in the school day when children can play

terrific (tuh-RIF-ik)—very good or excellent

whispered (WISS-purd)—talked very quietly or softly

Discussion Questions

1. Why do you think Sophie didn't welcome all the girls into her club?

2. How does it feel when someone doesn't let you be part of something?

3. Are you in any clubs? If so, what do you do in your club? If not, what kind of club would be interesting to you?

Writing Prompts

1. Pretend you are starting a club. Name your club and write three club rules.

2. Choose one character from the book and write a paragraph to describe her.

3. Make a list of things you know about Sophie's club. Then make a list about Katie's club. Compare the two clubs.

Katie Woo's Super Stylish Contest Winners!

Katie's special outfit in this book was designed by three Katie Woo readers. They were winners in a nationwide contest. The winning entries stood out for their creativity. Here are the winners:

Best Pant/Skirt
Erika Ahn, kindergarten
South Grove Elementary School
Syosset, New York

Best Accessories
Sophia Thibodeaux, grade 2
T. S. Cooley Elementary School
Lake Charles, Louisiana

Best Top
Jade Davis, grade 3
West Elementary School
Elvins, Missouri

Cooking with Katie Woo!

Club meetings are even more fun when members can share a snack. Here is a tasty, easy recipe. You could even make it a club activity and prepare it together. Make sure to ask a grown-up for permission and help if you need it!

Peanut Butter and Jelly Sushi

Ingredients:

- 1 loaf of sliced bread
- peanut butter
- jelly (flavor of your choice)

Other things you need:

- sharp knife
- rolling pin
- butter knife
- cutting board

What you do:

1. Cut the crusts from a slice of bread using the sharp knife.

2. With the rolling pin, flatten each strip of bread.

3. Use the butter knife to spread a layer of peanut butter on the bread. Repeat with jelly.

4. Starting at one end, roll up the bread. Repeat steps 1 through 4 with the rest of the bread.

5. Using the sharp knife, slice each roll into 1-inch pieces on the cutting board.

To make your treat extra special, serve the rolls on a pretty platter and try eating them with chopsticks!

THE FUN DOESN'T STOP HERE!

Discover more at www.capstonekids.com

- ♥ Videos & Contests
- ✿ Games & Puzzles
- ♥ Friends & Favorites
- ✿ Authors & Illustrators

Find cool websites and more books like this one at www.facthound.com. Just type in the Book ID: **9781479596393** and you're ready to go!